豬
Pig

鼠
Rat

牛
Ox

狗
Dog

虎
Tiger

雞
Rooster

兔
Rabbit

For nearly 5,000 years, the Chinese culture has organized time in cycles of twelve years. This Eastern calendar is based upon the movement of the moon (as compared to the Western which follows the sun), and is symbolized by the zodiac circle. An animal that has unique qualities represents each year. Therefore, if you are born in a particular year, then you share the personality of that animal. Now people worldwide celebrate this two-week-long festival in the early spring and enjoy the start of another Chinese New Year.

猴
Monkey

龍
Dragon

羊
Sheep

馬
Horse

蛇
Snake

To my father Henry and sister Brenda.
–O.C.

To Amy and Beckley, for all your love and encouragement!
– J.A.

immedium

Immedium, Inc.   P.O. Box 31846   San Francisco, CA 94131
www.immedium.com

Text Copyright ©2020 Oliver Chin
Illustrations Copyright ©2020 Jeremiah Alcorn

First hardcover edition published 2008.

Edited by Don Menn
Book design by Elaine Chu and Dorothy Mak
Chinese translation by Hsiaoying Chen, Grace Mak, and Dorothy Mak
Calligraphy by Lucy Chu

Printed in Malaysia
10 9 8 7 6 5 4 3 2 1

Library of Congress Cataloging-in-Publication Data

Names: Chin, Oliver Clyde, 1969- author. | Alcorn, Miah, illustrator.
Title: The year of the rat : tales from the Chinese zodiac / written by
   Oliver Chin ; illustrated by Miah Alcorn.
Description: [Revised edition.] | San Francisco : Immedium, Inc., [2020] |
   Parallel text in English and simplified Chinese. | Summary: Ralph the rat
   learns what his best qualities really are when his friend Bing needs help
   after a big bunch of balloons carries him away. Lists the birth years and
   characteristics of individuals born in the Chinese Year of the Rat.
Identifiers: LCCN 2019000142 (print) | ISBN 9781597021470 (hardcover)
Subjects: | CYAC: Rats--Fiction. | Animals--Infancy--Fiction. | Domestic
   animals--Fiction. | Astrology, Chinese--Fiction. | Chinese language
   materials--Bilingual.
Classification: LCC PZ10.831 .C61546 2020 | DDC[E]--dc23
LC record available at https://lccn.loc.gov/2019000142

ISBN 978-1-59702-147-0

THE YEAR OF THE RAT

Tales from the Chinese Zodiac

十二生肖故事系列 鼠年的故事

Written by Oliver Chin

Illustrated by Miah Alcorn

文：陈曜豪

图：艾尔康祖曼亚

WITHDRAWN

immedium
Immedium, Inc.
San Francisco. CA

As the sun peeked over the horizon,
Mama and Papa Rat cuddled their newest baby.
While his older brothers and sisters scampered
about, little Ralph opened his eyes and
let out a **"Squeak!"**

当旭日由地平线慢慢升起之际，
鼠爸爸和鼠妈妈抱起他们新生的小宝宝，
鼠哥哥和姐姐们乐得跑来跑去，
这时小洛夫睁开眼睛，然后轻叫了一声："吱！"

Papa scratched his chin, "This pup has spunk."

Mama smiled, "I'm sure the landlord's son will take a liking to you."

Sure enough, Bing heard the news and came to visit them in the attic.

鼠爸爸搔搔他的下巴说:"这小子好有胆量!"

妈妈笑笑:"我肯定主人的儿子一定会喜欢你的。"

果然,炳听到这个消息就走上阁楼去探望他们。

In his hand, Bing offered a piece of cheese. Ralph cautiously climbed aboard for a nibble and then a warm pet.

Soon, Ralph was running up Bing's arm, through his sleeves, and across his shirt.

他小心翼翼地爬上去轻咬了一口，
接着炳又给他温柔的拍抚。

不一会，洛夫就在炳的臂上遊玩，
穿过他的衣袖，横过他的衬衣！

Bing was tickled pink, "Let's go exploring!"

Nestling in, Ralph asked his parents, **"Can I go outside, please?"**

Mama replied, "Ok, but remember to watch your step and mind your manners."

炳玩得很开心，于是提议:"让我们出去探索下吧！"

偎依在炳的洛夫向父母请求道:"让我出去可以吗？"

妈妈回答:"好吧！但你要记着步步要小心，
还要注意你与人相处的态度。"

At the stables, Bing helped pitch the hay.
Ralph greeted the horses, **"Hello there!"**

But they snorted, "We can't be bothered
by small fries." Taken aback, he darted
and dodged their heavy hooves.

在马棚里，炳帮忙着推叠干草，
洛夫就和马儿问好说:"你们好！"

但他们嗤之以鼻说:"我们不要被那些小伙子骚扰。"
他吃了一惊退后闪避马蹄的重踏。

At the pens, Bing fed the pig and sheep. Ralph waved, **"Good day!"**

But they grunted, "Don't even think about tasting our food!"

Surprised by their behavior, he tried his best to stay out of their way.

炳在围栏里餵着猪和绵羊，洛夫挥手说:"大家好!"

但他们却咕噜说:"你别想吃我们的食物呀!"

被他们的行为吓惊了，
洛夫惟有尽量不去招惹他们。

Walking about the village, Bing gave his new pal some advice, "It's good to be friendly, but sometimes you need to mind your own business."

Ralph nodded shyly and fidgeted with his tail.

在村裡行走時，炳給他的新朋友一些忠告：
"对人友善是好，但有时候你需要少管閒事。"

洛夫羞怯地点点头及不安地盘弄着自己的尾巴。

That evening Mama asked,
"How was your trip, dear?"

那天晚上妈妈问他说："亲爱的，你的旅程怎样呀？"

Ralph answered, **"I wish it was easier to get along out there."**

洛夫答道："我希望出外时能够容易些与人相处！"

Papa replied, "Just keep your feet on the ground and your nose out of trouble."

爸爸回应："你记得要脚踏实地，勿惹事生非便行。"

Later, everyone settled down for the night.
But Ralph was still hungry and couldn't sleep.
He sniffed a tasty smell.

Curiously he followed the trail
down to Bing's kitchen.

稍后，大家都安顿下来过宿，
只有洛夫饥饿未能入睡，但他嗅到一股香味。

好奇心驱使下，他沿着小路走到炳的厨房。

"Waaa! What's this?" Bing's father turned on the light and saw Ralph sitting in a pile of cheese.

"Son, come fetch your pet!" frowned his dad, and the embarrassed boy carried Ralph back to bed.

"哗！这是什么？"炳的爸爸亮了灯，看到洛夫就坐在一堆乳酪里。

"儿子，把你的宠物带走！爸爸绉绉眉头，而尴尬的男孩就把洛夫带回去睡觉。"

At home, Mama Rat liked to gather odds and ends. She explained, "If no one is using it, I might need it someday."

Watching her pack her stuff, Ralph decided, **"I'll start my own collection."**

在家里，鼠妈妈喜欢收藏零碎的东西，她解释说：
"今天没有人用它，但有朝我可能用得上呢！"

看着妈妈收藏她的东西，洛夫也决定：
"我也开始收藏自己的。"

But one day, Bing's mother cried,
"Who took my earrings?"

有一天，炳的妈妈大喊："谁拿走我的耳环？"

After searching everywhere, Bing found
who had borrowed the shiny pearls.

经过四处寻找，炳终于发现谁借去这对闪亮的珍珠。

Nibbling his fingernails,
Ralph bashfully returned them.

洛夫咬着指甲含羞地退还耳环。

Meanwhile, Papa Rat liked to chew on anything handy.
Gnawing on a rope, he said, "Old habits are hard to break."

Ralph had inherited his father's teeth and guessed,
"I bet mine are sharp too."

同时鼠爸爸喜欢顺手拿到任何东西都放入口中嚼咬，
他啃着绳子一边说:"我就是积习难改！"

洛夫遗传了爸爸的牙齿，所以他猜想:
"我的牙齿也一样尖锐呢！"

The following day,
the dog lost his leash.

后来有一天，小狗失掉了狗带。

Next, the bucket dropped into the
well, and Bing's kite wouldn't fly.

跟着水井的吊桶跌入井里，
炳的风筝也断线不能飞上天空。

He discovered the reason why, and poor Ralph
promised, **"I will keep my mouth to myself."**

他发现原因就在小洛夫，小洛夫承诺："我一定会紧闭我的咀巴！"

But Bing's parents had enough. Their son's birthday party was tomorrow, and they didn't want any more problems from that little rat. They told a disappointed Bing to bring Ralph to the barn.

但炳的父母已经忍够了，明天就是儿子的生日会，他们不想见到这只小鼠再滋生事端，他们告诉失望的炳要把小洛夫送到壳仓去。

Putting Ralph in the rabbit cage, Bing whispered, "If you're good and stay here, you can go home tomorrow."

Ralph twitched his nose sadly as Bing shut the door and waved goodbye.

炳把洛夫放进兔笼里，
并叽哩他："乖乖的留在这里，
明天你便可以回家了。"

当炳关门与他挥手说再见时，
洛夫悲伤地抽搐着鼻子。

Outside the barn door, Ralph saw Bing's neighbors decorate the street.

He smelled cakes baking and heard people laughing.

Ralph moaned, **"Oh, I wish I could join the party, too!"**

在壳仓门外，洛夫见到炳的邻居在街上张灯结彩。

阵阵传来烤蛋糕的香气和人们的笑声。

洛夫闷哼说："噢！我真希望我也可以参加生日会！"

Finally Bing's birthday had come, and so did family
and friends. Presents arrived along with a big bunch
of balloons. They sparkled like every color of the rainbow.

炳的生日终于到了，他的家人和朋友也到了。
礼物随着一大束气球一起送来，色彩闪烁的气球有如一道彩虹。

Bing wanted to touch them all,

炳很想取下所有气球，

but suddenly their knot came loose.

但缚着气球的绳结突然松脱，

Fearing that the balloons would fly away,
he snatched their strings. "Whew!" he sighed.
However, the bunch kept pulling him up!

他怕气球会飞走，于是紧执着
气球的绳子，随着"咻！"一声惊叫，
只见那束气球把他拉上天空！

When his feet could no longer touch the ground,
Bing shouted, "Oh, rats!"

Everybody turned and gasped in alarm.
Quickly they tried to grab hold of him,
but he slipped through their grasp.

当他那双脚离地上升的时候，
炳大声呼喊："噢！不得了呀！"

在场每个人都恐慌地转身去抓他，
虽然人群很快就抓住了他，
但他却又从他们的手中溜走。

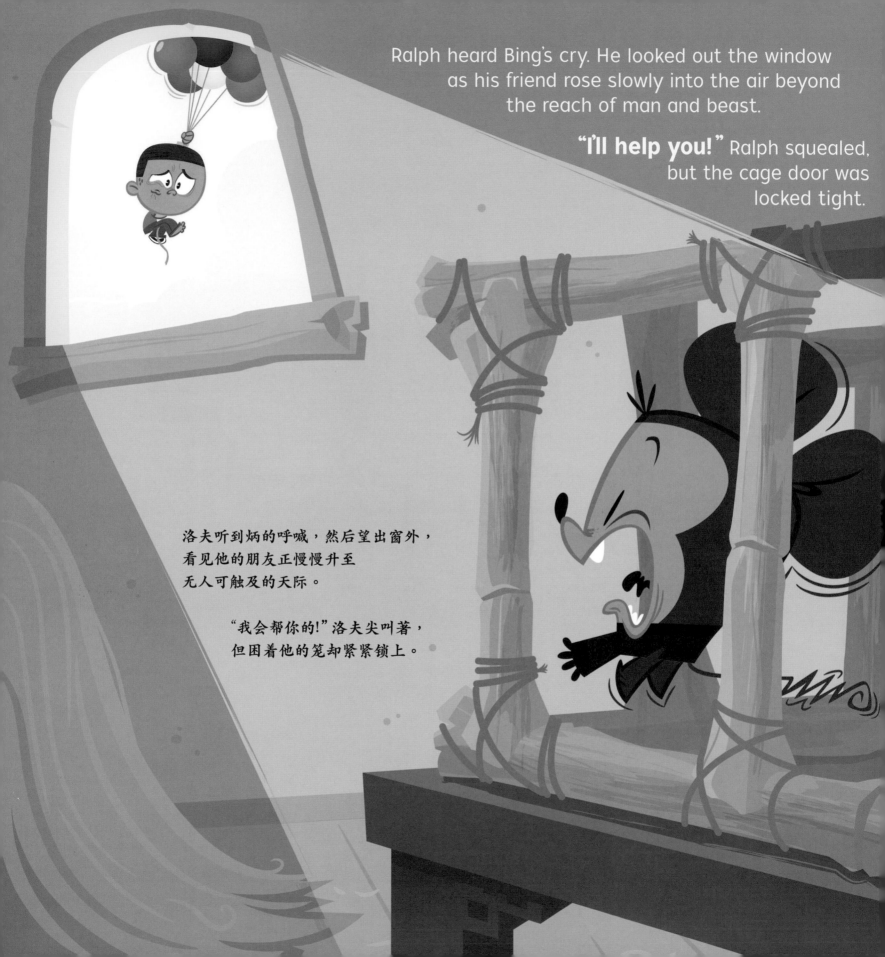

Ralph heard Bing's cry. He looked out the window as his friend rose slowly into the air beyond the reach of man and beast.

"I'll help you!" Ralph squealed, but the cage door was locked tight.

洛夫听到炳的呼喊，然后望出窗外，
看见他的朋友正慢慢升至
无人可触及的天际。

"我会帮你的!"洛夫尖叫著，
但困着他的笼却紧紧锁上。

Ralph anxiously scoured the floor for anything useful.
Then he rummaged through his pockets. **A-ha!**

He found a pin, reached around the bars, and jiggled
the lock open. He was free!

洛夫焦急着在地上到处寻找可用的东西，
然后又找遍他的口袋，啊哈！

他找到一根针，他拿着针越过闩栏，
轻轻摇动几下闩锁便打开，他自由了！

The rat bolted through a hole in the wall
and scaled the ladder to the hayloft.
Bing kept floating higher and higher.

On the ledge, Ralph took a deep breath,
closed his eyes, and jumped out!

老鼠穿过墙洞狂奔，再沿着阶梯爬上草寮，
炳则继续愈升愈高。

洛夫站在窗缘上，他深呼吸一下，
并闭上眼睛，然后一跃而下！

Boing! Boing! Resting on top of the bouncing balloons,
Ralph called down, **"Are you alright, Bing?"**

The boy looked up with amazement
and grinned, "Ralph,
I'm glad to see you!"

嘣! 嘣! 他跳在舞动的气球上，
洛夫向下大嚷:"炳，你还好吗？"

男孩惊讶地抬起头来，笑着说:
"洛夫，见到你真高兴!"

Scratching his head, Ralph squeaked,
"What should I do?"

They had soared above the trees and now
could almost touch the clouds. Bing hollered,
"I don't know, but think of something!"

洛夫抓着头皮尖叫："我该怎么办呢？"

他们已升到树顶上，眼见快要触及云端了。
炳烦恼地叫道："我不知道，但必须想个法子出来！"

Suddenly Ralph got an idea. He carefully
squeezed in between the balloons.

洛夫突然灵机一触想出法子来。
他小心翼翼地钻入气球之间。

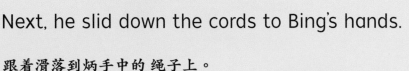

Next, he slid down the cords to Bing's hands.

跟着滑落到炳手中的 绳子上。

Then he began to bite through
the strings like a pair of scissors!

然后他开始像一把剪刀般去咬气球的绳子。

One after another, the balloons flew away, and the pair descended slowly towards the earth. In the meantime, they had drifted far from home.

Ralph decided, **"I think I see a place where we can safely land."**

气球一个接一个地飞掉，
这对朋友慢慢朝着大地降落，
但同时他们已飘离家居很远。

洛夫决定:"我猜想我看到
一个可以安全着陆的地方"

Skimming the treetops, Ralph cut the tie to one more balloon. **"Hold on tight!"** he hollered, as they braced for impact.

Wham! Bam! Luckily they had hit a soft spot... on the back of a startled ox!

掠过树顶后，洛夫再咬断
一个气球，并警告:"抓紧！"

他们紧紧抱在一起准备降落的冲击。
啪！砰！很幸运地他们降落在一个
柔软的地方...一只受惊的牛背上！

Hastily Ralph rummaged through his pockets again. He discovered a shiny earring and presented it to the wary stranger.

Happily she mooed in delight and agreed to take them home.

洛夫心急地再次往口袋里翻寻，真的给他找到一只闪亮的耳环，于是送了给这位陌生人。

接着开心地哞了一声答应送他们回家。

Back in the village, everyone was overjoyed at their return. Ralph sighed, **"I guess I'll go back to the barn."**

But everyone forgave him, since his ingenuity had come in very handy indeed.

他们回到村里,人人都为他们平安回家而乐透了,洛夫欸道:"我想我该返回壳仓。"

但每个人都宽恕了他,因为他的机智实在很有帮助。

Afterwards, Bing and Ralph
continued their travels.

The other animals and Bing's parents
didn't mind Ralph anymore.
They gladly let him scurry about
and share their belongings.

之后，炳和洛夫继续他们的旅游。

其他动物及炳的父母也不再与洛夫计较，
让他随处乱跑，和共用他们的东西。

Mama, Papa, and his brothers and sisters were rightly proud of Ralph.
This little rascal had a really big heart. And they all agreed
that it was an amazing Year of the Rat.

鼠爸爸、妈妈、和哥哥，姐姐们都为洛夫昂然自豪，因为这傢伙虽小，但勇气却不小！
最后大家都同意这是一个精彩的鼠年。

鼠

Rat
1924, 1936, 1948, 1960, 1972, 1984, 1996, 2008, 2020, 2032

People born in the Year of the Rat are ambitious, clever, and thrifty. They are nimble, optimistic, and sensitive. But sometimes they can be competitive and possessive. Though they may be nosy and a little thin-skinned, rats are truly resourceful and trusty pals!

在鼠年出生的人士，有志向、聪明和朴实。他们乐观而且灵敏，但有时他们可以很有竞争力和具有佔有慾。虽然他们或许会好管閒事及有点敏锐，不过老鼠确实是有机智並且是一位可靠的朋友！

Enjoy more fun bilingual stories by Ying Chang Compestine!

"Compestine's lively, original folktale is filled with action, noise, and humor, nicely captured in the detailed, cut-paper illustrations that resemb for read-alouds."